I0722708

Also by Luke Italiano

Geeky & Godly: Science Fiction, Fantasy, & Faith
Is it possible to be a geek and a Christian?
Can you be a fangirl and still love Jesus?
Spoiler Alert: Yes. Yes, you can!
Ages 10+

Hollow Heart
A handbook for any Christian struggling with depression, as well
as a guidebook for those who love someone with depression.
Here is hope. Depression doesn't have you. You have depression.
Jesus has you.

LUKE ITALIANO

THE BROKEN PROPHET

ELIJAH'S STORY

The biblical account of Elijah can be found in
1 Kings chapters 17 – 19 and 2 Kings chapter 2.

Chapter One

Black feathers fluttered from the pale blue sky and stuck to his sweaty forehead. He let them.

The raven landed on his shoulder, cawing around the bit of food in its beak. It dropped the morsel—a chunk of dried-up bread—and flapped away, leaving more feathers behind. The bread fell into his lap.

Elijah's eyes slid to the food. It lay cradled in the folds of his dust-colored robe. His stomach yawned, but he clamped his lips shut.

Unclean.

Still unclean.

God had said it was detestable. He had said ravens were detestable when he thundered on Mount Sinai hundreds of years ago. He'd said so to Moses, the great prophet who had come before. The same God who now mocked Elijah by sending the ravens to him every day. The same God who thought so little of him that he chose to feed him by birds that made whatever they touched unclean.

What had Elijah done? Why did God treat him with such contempt?

The stream gurgled below. At least he had good water. At least he had enough of that. And in this heat, he needed the water. Sweat dripped from his forehead. Finally, the feather fell from his forehead and wafted into his lap beside the chunk of bread.

Elijah stood, letting the food roll onto the baked earth. His knees cracked. Of course they did. Why wouldn't they crack? His back was sore, too. And it was hot out. The sun beat down on him. Not a cloud in the sky.

Complain, complain, complain, Elijah. At least you have water.

At least you have water.

He knelt down next to the muddy stream. It was really just a trickle these days. His knees shouted their protests again as he stooped down and dipped his hands into the water. The coolness flowed through his dusty fingers. He raised his hands and let drops fall back into the gurgling flow.

He pressed his lips together. No, Elijah. Don't do this. Not again. It's not worth it. Elijah, you are a prophet of the living God. Don't lose yourself again. Don't allow the darkness in your heart to wrap its arms around you. Not again.

No. The darkness came again. He wept.

It began as a sigh. It emanated from deep, deep within him. The sigh turned into a hum. The hum shifted into a sob. The sob became a wail.

Why?

Why would God do this?

Why would God punish him like this? Why would God force him to live in the wilderness, alone, under the cruel sun, being fed by unclean birds, day after day after day? Why would obedience result in a dark heart under the desert sun?

He'd done exactly what God had said. He'd gone to Ahab. He'd gone to the king and announced God's judgment. Ahab was the evil one. He's the one who had rejected God. He's the one who had led his entire nation away from the Almighty. He's the one who should be struggling with despair. He's the one who should be weeping.

No rain. That was God's judgment.

Ahab worshiped a rain god. See if that god could open up the sky. See if that god he worshiped could make the crops grow. Go ahead. Elijah's God was far more powerful. Being real helped with that.

And then.

And then God told him to come here. To be exiled from his people. To be alone.

His sobs slowed as he knelt there beside the brook. The water trickled past him, over the rocks, down the crevice he hid in.

Elijah heard the flapping. A weight pressed on his shoulder. It cawed.

Elijah roared as he spun, grabbing at the detestable creature. More feathers flew into his face. His hands met only air as they clawed after the bird. Cawing filled his ears.

Worthless.

He was worthless. Unclean. Forgotten by God at best. Probably being punished for something.

Maybe he should have tried harder with Ahab. Maybe he should have said something more. Maybe.

But now he sat in the desert by a stream.

Fed by birds.

Alone.

Was it the Sabbath?

Elijah furrowed his brow. He'd lost count of the days again, hadn't he? Weeks now. Months. No rain. No dew.

The land around him was dying. The grass on this slope was ready for burning. Even the brook was turning to mud.

His fault. He should have been smarter when he spoke to Ahab. He should have been better.

And again the raven lighted on his shoulder. Again it cawed. Again it dropped food. This time, a piece of meat. From what animal? Was it an unclean animal?

Did it even matter anymore?

He was worthless.

But here was food.

Here was food that God himself provided. Elijah didn't go get the food, did he? He couldn't. The king was probably trying to find him and kill him, even now. And he hadn't done anything that God should feed him.

But God was still feeding him, wasn't he?

Even after all his failures, even though Elijah wasn't enough, God took care of him. It was through these detestable creatures, yes. But still, the Almighty stooped to provide food for a failure like Elijah.

He reached for the piece of meat. Puffs of dust rose from his skin. So much dirt. It had been so long since he'd been able to wash.

He regarded the meat. Where had the meat come from? Direct from God, a miracle like the bread he'd provided in the desert for

Elijah's ancestors so many, many years ago? Or did the raven find it somewhere? Meat as unclean as the raven? Elijah didn't know. God didn't tell him these things.

God had told him to speak to Ahab.

And God had told him to hide.

And now God took care of him. Him. This worthless man. Now God provided in the desert.

Elijah brought the morsel to his mouth and chewed. Grit popped with the unidentified meat. Some sort of bird, perhaps? Impossible to tell. Tasteless, really. Either that or the omnipresent dust had canceled out Elijah's ability to taste anything. It might be that.

No, this wasn't a choice portion of any animal, but it was food. Food provided by Almighty God to a person who didn't deserve it.

Elijah swallowed the morsel.

The raven cawed and flew toward the sky. A feather landed in Elijah's lap.

He plucked the glossy black feather up. He raised his hands toward the sky. He prayed.

God was good to him. God had provided. Even in failure.

God was good to him. Even now.

God would remain faithful. He would provide. Elijah was certain. If he had done that so far, he wouldn't stop now.

And then the stream dried up.

Chapter Two

No one would be able to tell where Elijah ended and the dust began. The dust had become a texture that coated clothes and skin and grass and stream bed and even the sky. Where once water had flowed, only grit blew. The ravens had stopped coming. No more feathers. No more detestable animals.

Elijah missed the sound of their voices.

And in that place where grit coated even every thought, God spoke.

"Go at once to Zarephath in Sidon. Stay there. I have commanded a widow in that place to supply you with food."

Elijah blinked. Sidon?

His mind turned the word over. Sidon? The dirt around his eyes cracked as he thought.

Where was he now? He shook the dust from his mind. Kerith Ravine. That's where he was. The southeast corner of Ahab's kingdom. A place so far out of the way it was safe. Far from anyone.

But now God decided he needed to move to Sidon? Couldn't God just provide for him here, as he had been?

Elijah opened his mouth. His jaw creaked. Dirt fell from his face. He closed his mouth again. It would not do to question God. The Almighty had his reasons, didn't he? He wouldn't send him outside Israel's borders without a reason, would he? He wouldn't take him from this place of safety and place him in the home of Ahab's wife on a whim. No. God had to have some sort of plan.

And so Elijah stood. Dust showered off of his arms, his shoulders, his robe. The skin underneath was the same color as the dirt.

Time to walk.

The sun hurt his eyes as he looked over the hills of Israel.

The land was dying.

The ground was cracked. Broken. It should have been whole. There should have been barley growing now. Instead, the fields lay untilled. The men in the villages had a distance in their eyes. They sat at the city gates and around the wells. They did not greet Elijah as he passed by. They paid him no attention.

Every little town had an altar in it. Well-tended altars. All of them set up to the rain god that Ahab's wife had brought with her. A god named Baal.

It appeared that Baal wasn't listening.

On the roads, Elijah passed many travelers. Their skin was the same dust color his was. Their eyes held no hope. "I heard they had food in Egypt," one said.

"North. To Sidon," another answered.

"Across the sea," a third pointed.

Anywhere but here.

Rumors of food drove men and women to leave their land. What good was land when it could not feed you? What good was home without rain?

Elijah stepped into a nameless town on his journey. The sun dipped near the horizon. A cloud of dust seemed to follow the prophet. No men sat at the gate of the town. Perhaps they were attempting to get drunk on whatever they could find. Elijah plodded into the town and plunked himself down next to a well.

Some women stared at him. Each had a jar that could easily hold ten gallons. They were the same color as the dry land.

He smiled at them. The unfamiliar motion cracked the layers of dirt on his face. "Is there any water left?"

One of the women nodded.

"Please. May I have some?" What had happened to hospitality? The people of Israel were supposed to welcome guests, not ignore them. They should be offering water. But then again, if someone didn't worship God, why should they obey him?

The same woman nodded again and lowered her jar into the well, drawing out some precious, dripping liquid.

Elijah received the jar and held it to his mouth.

Oh.

He almost wept. It was so, so good to just hold the wetness in his mouth. He felt the cool flow down his throat. One swallow. Two.

Oh, Elijah, be careful. Too much and you'll make yourself sick.

He lowered the jar with shaking arms. He again smiled. He felt the dirt that had coated his beard no longer crack; now it simply oozed. Oh, it had been far, far too long since he had been able to wash.

Then again, the women looked no cleaner. Dirt creased around their eyes, their mouths.

He realized he was staring at them. He looked away quickly.

The women glanced at each other. He could hear them looking at each other.

One knelt by him. "It's been a long time since you've been to town," she said. She looked at him through dust-colored eyelashes. She took in his strange clothing: camel's hair tunic, wide leather belt. Her gaze shifted up to his face. She made eye contact.

Now Elijah simply nodded.

"A man like you must be lonely."

Elijah stood. "I must keep moving."

Another woman stepped closer. "Sir. If you wish, I am sure we might find a place for you to sleep." She smiled. Dust wrinkled at the corners of her mouth. "And anything else you might desire."

Elijah looked from one to the other. "You both are of age. You must have husbands!"

The one who still knelt stood and shrugged. "What of them? They spend all day at the shrine, praying for Baal to send rain. We need to make our money somehow."

Elijah scowled. He knew what praying to Baal meant. The temple prostitutes must be very busy in this drought.

The drought he'd caused.

If he had not prayed for God to shut the sky, if he hadn't given that message to Ahab, if he hadn't been so righteous for the Lord, these women might have their husbands. They might be happy. They might not be offering themselves to a stranger.

And gradually, his initial revulsion and anger turned to pity. Turned to guilt.

His fault, wasn't it?

He was the one who had closed the sky. He was the one who had driven the cities of Israel to such despair.

One of the women tried again. "If you prefer, I have a daughter who has not yet been with a man." She paused. "Or would you prefer my son?"

Elijah spent the night under the sky, away from town, alone. He slept in the dust.

The next morning he walked on to the north. The next night, he came to another village, another nameless town. Another dirty well. He had to get water himself here; no one would offer it to him. A few children walked the quiet streets. Elijah didn't want to think about the hungry, hungry children. Most of younger ones went around naked. He noticed most of the boys weren't circumcised.

God had commanded that the Israelites were to circumcise their boys eight days after birth. It was to set them apart. A physical mark of a spiritual reality.

But if the spiritual reality wasn't there, if they had turned their backs on God. Well. Why should they even pretend, then? Elijah felt an anger growing inside of him. Yes. Why even pretend? Yes, he had closed the sky at God's command, but these people deserved it. His people suffered, but they suffered because they'd turned their backs on the God who'd given them the land. How could they?

An old man wheezed nearby.

Elijah gestured toward the shrine he'd passed on the way into town. "What's happened to worshiping the God of Israel?"

The old man squinted. "What's happened to it? His shrine's right there!" he mumbled through toothless gums.

Elijah felt his face darken. "That's no shrine to the Lord."

"Oh! The Lord! Yes. We worship him, too. Sabbath's tomorrow."

"If the Lord is God, you should worship only him."

The old man laughed. "What fool would ignore worshiping Baal?"

Elijah finished his drink and stood. "Your rain god isn't making it rain, is he?"

"Well, we just need to worship harder." the old man squinted again. "You going up to the shrine to worship?"

"No."

And Elijah set his face toward Sidon.

Chapter Three

Zarephath.

The city had a wall the color of dust and a gate coated in dust. Its fields were filled with dust. All in all, it didn't seem much better than any of the towns he'd already passed through. It also didn't look any worse from this distance. Some people were out in the fields, so at least there was that.

Elijah stumbled down the road. Dirty and tired.

At least back by his stream with his ravens, he was rested. This was miles and miles now. Eighty-five miles he'd walked. Farther than an old man's bones liked to go, certainly.

And so much harder on his heart. Alone, he could imagine the people of Israel crying out against their king. He could dream that the people were turning back to God. Now, though? He thought he'd been broken before. He'd thought it was bad before. Now he knew the truth.

And now he had a new home outside Israel. At least wickedness here couldn't shock him. And perhaps, perhaps it wouldn't be so bad. God had told him there was a widow here to take care of him. Certainly, if there was a widow, there might be a bed. He let that thought roll around his head for a few moments. Oh, to lie in a bed again. And perhaps a pillow?

How would he find this widow?

As he drew nearer to the gate, he spotted a woman. Her face was toward the ground. She reached out a hand and snatched up twig after twig. Ah. She must be gathering firewood. Perhaps she was making food?

Elijah's stomach rumbled.

It had been a long time since the ravens had brought him food. So long since those unclean beasts had tormented him.

No. He didn't miss them. He shook his head at the thought with a slight smile.

He approached the woman. As he did, she glanced up at him, straightened, but then kept her eyes down. She seemed to brace herself.

Elijah tried talking, but only a croak came out. He cleared his throat. The dust coated everything, inside and out, didn't it? He tried again. "Would you bring me a little water so I could have a drink?" he asked. Perhaps they remembered hospitality here.

The woman sighed. How old was she? She couldn't be more than twenty. Her hair was still dark, but her eyes looked dead. Like many of the other women who had approached him on the journey.

The woman nodded and turned to go through the gate.

Elijah's stomach rumbled. If this was the woman, she should have food, right? "Please, bring me some bread, too?"

She turned back to him. "As surely as the Lord your God lives, I don't have any bread. I've got a handful of flour. I've got a tiny bit of oil." She held up the twigs in her hands. They trembled. "I was gathering wood for a fire to bake it. I'm going to feed it to my boy, and then we're going to die." She wrinkled her nose at him.

Going to die?

Thoughts thundered through Elijah's head, shoving through the dirt that had become his mind.

How dare he ask? How dare he ask, in the midst of a drought, that a woman give him so much?

But God had said. The same God who had given him enough at the brook. The God who had provided, even through those ravens. And God said now . . . He said the widow would provide.

And God kept his promises. He always kept his promises. He'd fed Elijah before. He'd feed him now.

Elijah cleared his throat again, dirt grinding as he spoke. "Don't be afraid. Do what you just said. But first make me a little bread. And then bake some for you and your son. This is what the God of Israel says: 'The jar of flour won't be used up, and the jug of oil won't run dry. Not until my God gives rain on the land.'"

The woman raised an eyebrow.

The God of Israel shouldn't have any power here. This was Sidon. This was where Baal ruled. This was where Baal decided when it would rain.

And then it struck Elijah. The woman had known. She had named the God he served—not Baal, but the Lord. She'd said as much. How did she recognize him? How did she know Elijah served this God from the south?

But with her raised eyebrow, she turned and went into the city. Elijah waited by the gate.

Men of the city gathered there to do business. One man in a purple-dust colored robe approached. "What brings you here? Business?"

Elijah coughed. "I'm visiting. Just passing through."

"If you need a place to stay, I would be happy to welcome you." The man bowed. "My home is marked for its hospitality."

"Thank you, but I have already arranged a place to stay." Elijah bowed back.

Before long, the woman returned. She frowned as she handed him a still-hot fist-sized loaf of bread and a jug of water.

The man raised both eyebrows. "Is this the woman you await?"

Elijah didn't answer as he raised the jug to his lips, letting some water splash out down his beard.

The man chuckled. "You are sure to have a pleasant stay."

The woman glared at him but did not answer. She merely turned and stalked away.

Elijah broke off a piece of the loaf and inhaled. Oh. Fresh-baked bread. It had been so, so long. He put the piece in his mouth and chewed, savoring the texture, the taste. He attempted to not weep.

"Shouldn't you be following her?" the man asked, watching as the widow left.

Elijah shrugged. "I'm sure she'll return when she is ready to host me. For now, I'm happy with water and bread."

"Well, when you've had your way with her, come find me. The name is Belavi. Many know be by my trade." He smoothed the distinctive purple fabric he wore. "While I'm sure I cannot match her wiles, my conversation will be far more entertaining."

"Who is she?" Elijah asked.

"A widow."

Elijah pressed his lips together, awaiting more information.

"She was married to a man who was not the father of her child. He died of a wasting disease. Clearly a result of her wandering ways. Baal wanted revenge." Belavi shrugged. "She does what she can to get by now, but drought makes those who are cursed by the gods that much worse off."

Elijah nodded.

Of course it would be this way. He had hoped this widow would be a faithful old woman, perhaps attempting to escape those who had rejected God in Israel. But no. God wouldn't do that. From unclean birds feeding him to an unclean woman feeding him.

The sun crept closer to the horizon. At last, the widow returned.

Her eyes had softened. "Follow me, man of God."

And so Elijah found a home at last with an unclean woman and her son.

Chapter Four

She led Elijah through the streets of Zarephath without a word. Those still in the streets at this late hour whispered as they passed by. At last, they came to an old two-story structure like most of the buildings inside the city walls. A young boy, perhaps four years of age, sat in the doorway. His eyes were as hollow as his mother's. When he spotted Elijah, he sighed and began walking out of the doorway.

"No, Rahim. He is not a customer." Her words were tired.

A smile sprouted on the boy's face. He toddled back into the house.

Elijah raised an eyebrow.

She looked to the ground. "There is little a woman can do to earn her bread."

"You will not have to do that again. Not as long as I am here." Elijah's voice was still rusty. "Did you eat?"

She nodded.

"There was enough oil?"

"And enough flour."

"And neither will run out until there is rain. God has promised."

Her eyes searched the ground, unsure what to do.

"What is your name?"

"Amrah."

Elijah waited. The sky turned darker. Somewhere, people shouted. Somewhere else, people laughed. Here, though, Amrah said no more.

"I am Elijah."

After a long moment, she said, "Elijah. Come. I will take care of you until you leave."

Elijah insisted on sleeping in the kitchen. Amrah and her son slept upstairs. At dawn, she entered the kitchen and stirred the fire. Elijah heard a sharp gasp.

"This was empty last night. Twice." She brought a rough stone jar to where Elijah sat. She shook it in his face. "Empty. There was no flour left."

The prophet peered into the jar. Coarse white powder floomfed toward him. He winced away before the powder could coat his cheeks. He gave a dry cough. "How much bread will that make?"

"Two loaves." Amrah looked up at him. "Enough for the three of us today."

Elijah nodded. "God has promised." It was so easy to say it to someone else.

Amrah emptied the flour jar and the oil jar. Soon the scent of fresh bread filled the kitchen. Elijah sat back and closed his eyes, breathing in the aroma.

Perhaps Zarephath would be better than the ravine after all. At least the smell would be better.

Elijah sat on the roof, basking in the early morning sunlight before it got too hot. He closed his eyes and lifted his hands to the south.

The boy came up the stairs and watched. "What are you doing?"

Elijah creaked open an eye and sighed. "Praying."

The boy peered around the roof. "Practicing praying?"

"No. Praying."

"You didn't bring anything to give to a god. Why should he listen?"

Elijah smiled. "I don't have to bring him anything. He will listen anyway because he loves me." Today he could believe it. Today there were flour and oil. Today he was safe.

The boy wrinkled up his nose. "Gods don't love people."

"Gods don't, because there aren't gods."

The boy shrugged. "So who are you praying to?"

"The Lord."

The boy shrugged again and trundled away.

And so it was. Every day, enough oil and flour for the three of them. Every day, Amrah used up every bit of it. Every day, they ate.

And every day Elijah prayed.

He looked south toward his home. Beyond his home. Farther south, to the city of Jerusalem. To the temple. The place where the

Lord dwelled. Was it better there? What was happening at home? How bad was it?

How bad was it that God had sent him here, so far away? Weren't there any widows there who needed this miracle?

Were there any left who worshiped? Was Elijah the last?

The thought became a presence in his heart. The last one. After him, there would be none. None would worship the true God. And who would hold back his fury then?

He must do something. But what? He had shut the sky. What more could a prophet do? He was no Moses who could divide the sea. He was no David who could lead in battle. No. Elijah was worthless. Not even worthy of staying in his nation anymore. And so the darkness rooted in his heart, though some days he could beat it back. Some days, the sun warmed him. Some days, he believed God truly could love him.

Ah, but some things happened every day.

Every day, the boy asked questions. Every day, Elijah answered with more confidence than he felt.

Every day, Amrah offered for Elijah to sleep upstairs. She and Rahim could sleep in the kitchen. Every day, Elijah declined.

Every day, Elijah watched as Amrah left her home. She went to pray at the temple. Little Rahim went with her. "Come with us," the boy begged. He still knew how to smile, and his smile pried at Elijah's heart.

Elijah shook his head. "No. I will not pray to someone as powerless as Baal."

Amrah wouldn't answer. She walked away without a word. Rahim followed, looking back at the prophet over and over again.

Elijah would watch everyone go to the temple. It seemed he was the only one who prayed to the south. He was the only one who looked to the Lord.

He was alone. Even though he lived in a home now, even though the Lord provided him bread, even though the feathers of detestable birds no longer fluttered down on him, he was still alone. Surrounded by a foreign people in a foreign land. Why wouldn't he be alone? He was the last.

Chapter Five

Amrah insisted. Rahim begged. Finally, Elijah assented. He was given the upper room, and Amrah and her son moved into the kitchen. There was a window in his room that looked south. He wouldn't need to pray on the roof anymore.

Every day, fresh bread. Every day, the other two went to the temple. Every day, Elijah prayed. Every day, Rahim asked more questions.

"Why do you have a beard?"

"Why can't you pray at the temple?"

"Why did Baal leave?"

"Why do you have that weird clothing?"

"Why don't you pay for mom?"

Question after question after question.

And then one day, he began coughing.

Elijah prayed for the boy.

The boy got worse. His coughing grew deeper. His voice became a whisper.

Still, he asked questions.

"Why do people get sick?"

"Wasn't I praying hard enough?"

"Why aren't you at your home?"

One day he didn't go to the temple to pray. "Watch him," Amrah said.

Elijah did. The boy didn't get up from his spot near the oven. His voice was rough and sleepy, but the questions continued.

"Why do people get sick?"

"Why aren't you praying with mom?"

"Why doesn't anyone like mom?"

Elijah answered the boy as well as he could: Because the world is broken. Because he prayed to a God who was real. Because . . .

Elijah didn't want to answer that last question.

"Am I going to die?"

Elijah breathed in and out. The boy breathed in and out. He blinked so, so slowly at the prophet. He waited.

Elijah looked away. "I don't know."

"If I die, what will happen to me?"

That little boy. That Rahim. He looked up at Elijah. He had crust in his eyes. He coughed. He waited.

Elijah paced the room. He licked his lips. "My God takes all who trust him to a glorious place. A place where nothing is broken."

"Is there still a drought there?"

"No."

"What is it like? To not have a drought?"

Elijah groaned as he sat down near the child. "It means there is rain."

"Mom told me about rain before. I think she misses it."

"I think we all do."

The boy was silent for a while. One of the coals in the oven popped. "Elijah?"

"Yes?"

"I don't believe in your God. I believe in Baal."

"I know."

"But your God's place sounds nicer than mine."

"I think so."

"Can I believe in your God? Is that allowed?"

The boy was a foreigner. He was not of God's people. He wasn't circumcised. That was the sign of the covenant, wasn't it? That special gift given to Abraham to show that a person belonged to the God of Abraham. The true God.

Elijah clenched his fists.

Amrah shuffled into the room from the street. "How is he?"

"Inquisitive."

She took her place next to him. Elijah watched for a moment. The room smelled of warm bread and despair. He went upstairs to pray.

The next day, Amrah asked Elijah to sit with the boy again. The child labored in his breathing. He complained of the cold. He didn't ask a single question.

Amrah returned and sat by his side, keeping vigil.

Elijah went to his room to pray. Again, he prayed for the boy.

The next day, the boy didn't complain of being cold. He lay near the oven. His breathing was shallow. Amrah held his hand. The jar of flour and the jar of oil were full, but she did not bake any bread that day.

At dawn, Elijah came down to the kitchen. Amrah sat leaning against a wall, holding Rahim's hand in her own. The woman did not stir as the prophet entered the kitchen. In the quiet of the morning, Elijah merely looked on them.

The boy was resting so peacefully. Perhaps the fever had broken at last. Elijah attempted to hold back grateful tears.

He was not successful.

Amrah stirred. She groaned as she sat up from the wall.

And then she stopped. She stared down at her son's hand.

And she wailed.

Elijah jumped in surprise. He rushed to her side. Amrah shoved him away and huddled over her boy. "He's dead!"

No.

No. It could not be. He was so still!

He was so still.

And now Elijah's tears joined Amrah's.

The woman looked up at him and snarled. "What do you have against me, man of God? You came here to remind me of my sin and kill my son, didn't you?"

Elijah felt his hands curl into fists. "No." The word was cold. Hard. "Give me your son." He gathered the boy in his arms and lifted.

Oh.

The boy was so, so light. Elijah almost dropped him. His skin felt unnatural. Elijah carried him up the stairs to his room. Carefully, carefully he laid the boy on his bed.

And he prayed.

At first, no words came. He opened his mouth, and no sound came out but a wailing. He vomited out all the darkness in his heart in that wail. All the despair, all the anger, all the uncertainty, all the doubt, all of it came roaring out of him. Finally, his wail died. Finally, he was hollow. Finally, the words came.

"Lord. My God. Did you do this? Did you make this widow's son die? Did you bring this tragedy on her?" The words were so, so bitter.

Things were finally better. He was finally comfortable. He might be in a pagan city, living with pagan people, but no one was trying to kill him. He was safe. He had a bed. He had food. And now this child had to die? Why? Why would such a thing have to happen? The rage began to grow in him again. The darkness had not fled in that roar.

He took the boy's hand in his own. His cold, cold hand. The prophet bent over the child. His body shook with sobs. A form that small should not be that cold. He lay on the boy, willing his warmth to go into the boy. He stood. Paced. He shook as he sucked in breath. He lay on the boy again. Paced. Lay on him a third time.

This should not be. The boy had done nothing. His mother perhaps had. No, she had sinned. Even she recognized it. But the boy? Rahim had done nothing! He was even reaching out to the God of Abraham!

But now it was too late. There were stories of miraculous healings in the history of Elijah's people. But this boy was beyond healing.

But his God could do the impossible, couldn't he? His God had made the world with just words. He had knit this boy together in his mother's womb. The God who had created this body could bring it back to life, couldn't he?

"O Lord! My God!" Elijah shook. "Let this boy's life return to him!" And all that darkness again shot out from him toward his God. Except now, it was not just despair.

His God clung to him. Even as Elijah shook, even as he railed, even as he pushed away, his God loved him enough to hold on to him.

The Lord heard Elijah's cry.

Rahim coughed. He curled up on the bed, coughing, coughing, reaching for breath. And then he opened his eyes. He looked around. He breathed in, filling his lungs so, so full. And then he smiled. "I'm hungry," he said.

Elijah's roar turned into a laugh. With a shout, with a joyous shout, he gathered up the boy in his arms and squeezed.

"Why are you laughing?" he asked.

Elijah found his breath. "Oh, Rahim! Oh!" And he could say no more. Tears rolled down his cheeks. He looked up toward heaven and shouted praise.

"What are you doing?"

Elijah grinned through his tears at the boy. "Let's ask your mom to make some bread."

Chapter Six

Amrah sobbed as she clutched her son. She rocked him, heaving with the same tears Elijah had shed. "Now I know." She paused as another cry shook her. "Now I know you are a man of God. Now I know that the word of the Lord from your mouth is the truth." She buried her face in her son's neck, breathing in his scent, taking in the fact that he was alive, *alive*, and that he was her son and he had not left her.

She made bread for her son and Elijah. The oil and flour were waiting for her. She watched Rahim eat every bite.

He asked all the questions. "Why did I die? How did I come back? Why didn't Baal answer your prayers? Why aren't you eating?"

Amrah grinned at every question with watery eyes.

She didn't go back to the temple of Baal again, at least while Elijah stayed with her. Instead, she sat at his feet. And now it wasn't just Rahim asking questions. She asked questions about his God. Any God who would give her child back, despite what she had done, despite the guilt that clawed at her—a God like that was better than Baal who ignored her cries for rain and a husband and so many other things.

Rahim sat quietly and listened as Amrah and Elijah talked.

Well, not so quietly.

Not quietly at all, really.

"Why did Eve take the fruit?"

"Is there enough water to make a flood?"

"When will the Messiah come?"

Rahim watched Elijah pray. He listened closely. Soon, he prayed, too. He faced south toward Jerusalem. He prayed for the people there.

Amrah learned to smile over the next months. Rahim grew. Many of the children he played with in the streets did not grow nearly so well. Many of the adults became hollow-eyed. Amrah, though, had food enough and a new source of joy.

About a year after Elijah's arrival, he circumcised Rahim.

Elijah learned to smile, too. Amrah was like a daughter to him, and Rahim like a grandson. They talked long, long into the night. At last, he was not alone. At last, someone else worshiped the true God with him. His heart felt like it had at last become whole. The darkness retreated.

Most days, anyway.

When Elijah knelt to pray facing Jerusalem, he wondered. What happened in Israel now? Had they repented yet? Had Ahab learned to turn away from Baal?

So, in prayer, the darkness would seep from his heart and lash at him. Prayer became a sorrow. A reminder of what he left behind. A memory of all those who had forsaken the one true God. He was alone. The last prophet. The last one who trusted.

Except for Rahim. Except for Amrah.

But they were not of Israel, were they? They were still foreigners. They still did not belong, even if they did believe. So what did that make them?

What did that make Elijah?

Three years. Three years since Elijah had told Ahab it would not rain. Three years of hardship. Three years of dust.

And the word of the Lord came to Elijah. "Go and present yourself to Ahab. I will send rain on the land."

And so Elijah bid farewell to the joy he had found in Zarephath. Amrah clung to him. Rahim clutched his legs.

"Why do you have to go?"

"Why is God taking you from us?"

"Why can't you just stay?"

"Take my son," Amrah said. "There's nothing for him here. Take him with you."

Elijah looked down at the boy. He was so young yet, but he had grown.

Could he?

Should he?

"You will need someone to bake your bread," Amrah said. "You don't know how."

"I do, too!"

"You haven't once baked bread in all the time you've been here."

Elijah harrumphed. "Fine. I will take him."

The boy cheered. It took him only minutes to gather his few belongings.

"Take care of him," she implored the prophet.

"I will." The darkness peeked from his heart. He shoved it back down.

The boy returned and rushed into his mother's embrace. "Mom, are you going to see other men again?"

"No. Never again."

"How will you get bread?"

"I will have enough oil and flour until it rains. God has said so."

"Is anyone ever going to like you again?"

She smiled down at him. Elijah recognized the sadness behind her eyes. His darkness felt the same way all too often. She finally answered, "I do not need to worry about whether or not they like me. God loves me. That is enough."

"Is it?"

"Yes, Rahim."

And Elijah recognized that tone, too. Words that she knew were true, even if she could only barely grasp their truth and hold on to them herself. Oh, he knew what that was like all, all too well.

Amrah gave them each a cake of bread for the road, still warm from the oven. "Go with God."

Elijah smiled through tears. "God sent me to you. Now he sends me away. You have blessed me. Thank you."

Amrah simply smiled back. She watched for a long, long time as the prophet and her son set out to the south. For Israel.

Chapter Seven

Home.

God had told Elijah's ancestors it was a land flowing with milk and honey. The hills were covered with green every time it rained.

The corners of Elijah's eyes crinkled as he told Rahim, "Oh, there's nothing quite like walking on the fresh grass in bare feet." He grinned. "And the palm leaves just waving in the wind. You could come up over a rise like this one and look down at all the green, waving at you like a long-lost friend. And now. Finally. I'll be home." He breathed in as if he could inhale the aroma of fresh palm.

They topped the rise and looked down into the valley.

The color of dust. Dry as tinder. Nothing moved. Nothing waved. The rocks themselves seemed to cry out for water.

Elijah pressed his lips together. It was a ruin. But it was home. At least, that's what he told himself. And why should he be surprised?

Israel had withered even more in his years away, and no wonder. More than three years without rain left so many hungry. As bad as it had been when he'd journeyed to Zarephath, it must be so, so much worse now. But if God was sending him back, perhaps the nation had repented at last. Perhaps.

And no matter what, it ended soon. God had said so. The rain would return. And that began with confronting the king. That began with facing down the one who had turned away from God. And then—Elijah smiled— then the green would return.

Rahim looked up at him. "Why are we stopping?"

He stopped after only one question. He must be so very tired.

"I am enjoying what I am seeing."

The boy peered out at the valley. "Rocks?"

"My rocks."

They made their way down into the valley.

"What are we doing here?" Rahim asked. His words dragged from his lips. He stumbled over a rock.

"See that man there?" Elijah pointed ahead on the road. In the distance wavered the image of a man. He had a long white beard and no hair on top of his head.

"Yes?"

"We're here to talk with him."

"Who is he?"

Elijah forced a smile. "Obadiah. An old friend. He works for the king, but he serves God."

They kept walking, their feet scritching on the gravel of the path. The sun glared white down at them, reflecting off the bare stones.

As the man came near, he paused to speak in greeting. Elijah and Rahim returned the greeting. The man offered a shallow bow to them and then paused again. He looked up at Elijah's face, his eyes squinting, searching. And then the man fell on his face.

"Is it you? Is it really you, my lord Elijah?"

Elijah chuckled. "Yes! And go. Go tell your master that Elijah is here."

The man looked up from the ground. "What? Why? What have I done wrong?"

Elijah's smile died on his lips.

The man got up from the ground. "Are you trying to kill me? The king has sent emissaries to every kingdom under the sun looking for you. Elijah, he has turned this kingdom upside down." His voice thickened. He paused before continuing. "And if I go and tell him you're here, and God takes you away like he did three years ago, what will Ahab do to me?" He glanced back the way he had come, as if he'd be able to see the king. "Hasn't God told you what I've done? I've been hiding prophets, Elijah. The queen's been trying to kill them all, but I've been able to keep them safe. One hundred of them. I feed them. I'm even able to get them water. After three years without rain, I still get them water! And now you want Ahab to kill me? After all I've done?"

Elijah waited until the words ran as dry as the land. Finally he said, "Does God live?"

Obadiah blinked. "Of course."

"As surely as the Lord lives, I will present myself to Ahab today. Today, old friend. Today." His voice was steel. He would not allow Obadiah to be punished. Elijah wasn't enough. He was the one who had failed, hadn't he? But Obadiah had been faithful in all Israel, apparently. Someone had not forgotten God. And Elijah would not see him punished for that.

Obadiah placed a hand on Elijah's shoulder. Its sudden weight shocked Elijah. "Will it end, then? Is God finally going to end it?"

Elijah grinned. "The nightmare will finally be over. Our nights of tears will end." And of that he was certain.

The end was coming at last.

Ahab rode out to meet him. Not in a chariot. Not on a mighty charger. On a donkey. On a shaggy animal, a beast of burden.

Elijah chuckled as he saw it. Not even the king could maintain a good military in this drought. Not even a noble steed for his own use. Even the king was brought low.

Good. He deserved it. After his stubbornness had made an entire nation thirst. After all he had done. After all he had made Elijah do. After all he'd made Elijah feel. The shame of being unclean. Running away.

It all ended now. All of it.

Ahab dismounted. "There you are. Troubler of Israel."

"Me?" Elijah's voice was low. It shook. "Me? I'm the troubler of Israel?" And now his voice became a snarl. The darkness in his heart lashed out. No. Not this time, king. He wasn't the one who'd caused the trouble. True, he hadn't been enough. He wasn't good enough to do what actually needed to be done. But he wasn't the one who had caused the trouble. "Not me. You. Your father's family. You've done this. You rejected God. You seized on the Baals. But enough. Let's end this. I will meet you on Mount Carmel. Bring with you all the prophets of Baal you have. Four hundred fifty, is it? And bring the prophets of Asherah that your wife feeds. All four hundred of them. Let's see, Ahab. Let's see who the troubler of Israel is."

Chapter Eight

Mount Carmel.

Once, an altar of God had been there. Simple, unfinished stones piled high to receive sacrifices given to God. Once, God's people had gathered there to worship. Ahab himself had seen it desecrated. Destroyed. He'd laughed at how impotent their God was. He couldn't even protect his own altar.

Now God was going to reclaim what was his own.

Elijah could almost see the thoughts churning in Ahab's mind. Certainly his feelings about Elijah and the God he served were no secret. The king's eyes lit with excitement, surely picturing Elijah's defeat. Picturing this old religion dead and buried. Picturing the rain that would return to the land once more.

So Ahab did all Elijah had said. He gathered up his prophets. Made sure they were ready for this showdown. As all the prophets, the great crowd of them, marched from the palace in Samaria, ready to do battle with the prophet who dared oppose them, a crowd gathered.

And the crowd followed. It seemed like the entire city followed.

It wasn't like they had anything better to do. They couldn't care for crops that were dead anyway. They might as well follow and see what had bothered Ahab so much. They passed through a nearby town. People there joined the train. And more and more. As they marched the miles to Mount Carmel, the followers grew to a great multitude.

Muttering spread through the crowd. A showdown between Ahab and the prophet who defied him? A battle between gods? They had never seen anything like that. It would be entertaining, if nothing else.

Ahab grinned. "Good. Let them all see the fall of Elijah. Let them see what this weakling God is worth."

The breeze blew cool off the ocean and onto the mountain. The sea's great blue expanse vanished into a horizon that blended with the sky. Dawn broke in the east, behind the mountain, opposite the sea. A mound of stones, neglected for years, lay before the crowd. And there Elijah, his great beard fluttering in the wind, his face bathed in the orange light of dawn, held up his arms for attention. "Still don't believe? If Baal is so good, why can't he send rain? If the Lord is God, follow him! But if Baal is God, follow him!"

The multitude did not answer him. A few dared make eye contact. Most simply awaited the spectacle.

Ahab sat on a camp chair that had been brought for him. He gloated.

Elijah lowered his arms and shook his head. "I'm the only one of the Lord's prophets left. Look! Four hundred and fifty of these prophets for Baal! But let's see whose god is more powerful. Get two bulls. Bring them here. I'll prepare my bull for sacrifice, but I won't light it on fire. You do the same. You call on the name of your god, and I'll do the same. Let's see who answers with fire."

The people answered, "What you say is good!" What should they care which god answered? All they cared about was some entertainment. And with the cool breeze, at least it was comfortable here.

Elijah looked at those other prophets. Those fakes. "Set up your altar. Prepare the bull. Don't set it on fire. Let's see what happens," he spat.

And so the prophets of Baal took a bull and prepared it. They set up their altar.

And they prayed.

Over four hundred of them prayed. They bowed. They stretched their hands up to the sky. They chanted. They shouted. They danced.

Rahim watched. "This is what my mother did at the temple. Except for the naked people. Are they going to be naked here?"

Elijah shifted. "Perhaps. I hope not."

The boy cocked his head. "No one ever answered there."

"No one will answer here," Elijah replied.

"What happens if no one answers you?" Rahim asked.

Elijah pressed his lips together. "The Lord will answer."

"How do you know?"

"He has told me."

"What's that pile of rocks? Are those your rocks, too?" Rahim pointed.

Elijah sighed. "No. Those are God's rocks. It was his altar once."

Rahim's eyes flickered between the desecrated altar and the prophet's craggy face. He didn't ask any more questions for a while.

The sun rose higher. The light turned from gentle orange to bright white. The watching crowds made themselves comfortable on the ground, taking in the spectacle. Moisture beaded on Elijah's forehead and ran down his face and into his beard. The air grew heavy with the scent of sweat.

Rahim continued to watch. "How long will they go?"

"Long enough to prove no one listens."

At noon, Elijah called out, "Shout louder! Baal probably just can't hear you. Surely Baal is a god! Maybe he's thinking too hard to hear you!"

Rahim giggled beside him.

The prophets ignored the haranguing. They shouted louder. They danced harder.

Elijah winked at the boy and called out again, "Perhaps he's busy relieving himself! You know how much noise Baal makes then! He just can't hear you over that!"

Rahim giggled in delight.

"Oh! He must be sleeping! You know how loud he snores!"

Rahim didn't giggle as hard at that one. Elijah shrugged. Some children had no taste.

But now the prophets took out swords and spears. They cut themselves. They let their blood splatter the altar. Now it smelled of iron. Their god must pay attention to that. Look how serious his prophets were! Look how much they trusted him! Look what they were willing to give, if he would only answer!

The sun began to descend.

There was no response. No fire from heaven. Not even a whisper of it.

No one answered.

No one paid attention.

It was time for the afternoon sacrifice in the Temple far to the south in Jerusalem. A good time to offer a sacrifice here.

Elijah rose from where he crouched. "Enough." He shook his head at the four hundred fifty prophets of Baal. "Enough. Your god is not answering. If he could, he would have already."

Their bloody faces showed anger, shock, despair. Blood dripped from their fingers. Flies buzzed around the unburned slaughter on their altar. Some thought to protest, but most simply fell into sitting positions, exhausted by the day. They breathed hard and looked up at him, daring him with their expressions to do better.

He turned to the multitude of watchers. "Come here to me." His voice was low but held flint within it. These people would see the power of the God they had been so indifferent to.

And there, under their eyes, he repaired the ruined altar of the Lord. He took twelve stones—one for each of their tribes—and he built the altar. He looked around. "Rahim. Does someone have a shovel?"

The boy stood there for a moment but then scampered off. He soon returned, bearing a spade.

Elijah took it from him and dug. He groaned; his bones had become accustomed to simply sitting these last years. The sweat poured off of him, even in the cool air of the mountain. At last, his labor was finished: a trench encircled the restored altar.

He took wood and laid it atop the altar. He took the bull and prepared it, slaughtering it, separating the pieces, placing them on the altar. Rahim watched every move closely.

And then Elijah looked again to the crowd. "Get me some water."

The crowd brought four jars filled with water. Large jars.

"Pour it over the sacrifice."

And so they did.

"Do it again."

They ran down to the sea to fill up the jars and returned, pouring the water over the sacrifice.

"A third time."

And so it was done.

The water ran down the carcass, down the wood, down the stone, down to the trench. So much water, the trench filled. The ground couldn't drink the water in fast enough.

Elijah heaved a deep breath. He prayed. "O Lord, God of Abraham, Isaac, and Israel, let it be known today that you are God in Israel and that I am your servant and have done all these things at your command. Answer me, O Lord. Answer me so these people will know that you, O Lord, are God, and that you are turning their hearts back again."

The clear blue sky answered with fire.

The heat of the blast pressed against Elijah's cloak, sending it fluttering. The sweat on his face evaporated in a heartbeat. Flames swallowed up the sacrifice. The altar. The water in the trench. Everything. It was all gone.

God had taken it all.

And the people cried out: "The Lord! He is God! The Lord is God!"

Chapter Nine

The prophets of Baal stared at the crater where once there had been an altar. The ground shimmered like a great glass bowl. Their own altar lay behind them, forgotten.

And Elijah turned to them. "Grab them."

The people rose up as one and seized the prophets. Elijah had them dragged down to the valley. He would not desecrate a place holy to the Lord with their blood. Well, not more than they had already spilled themselves.

After it was done, Elijah breathed hard. His own hands were now bloody, as were his feet and the hem of his robe. But it was done. Those prophets would never mislead another again. God's judgment had fallen.

Now it was time to find Ahab. The man who had allowed the prophets of Baal to rule. The one who had hunted down God's own prophets. The king who had misled Israel. The wicked one who had tried to kill Elijah. Who had named him the troubler of Israel. Judgment must land on him as well.

But it was not time for Ahab to die. Not yet.

Elijah was going to embarrass him first. "Go. Eat. Drink."

Ahab's face was a thundercloud of anger. His prophets destroyed. He himself shamed before his people. And now Elijah was telling him to celebrate?

But Elijah's deadly grin did not allow Ahab a chance to speak. "Do you hear the heavy rain coming?"

Yes. The prophets of the rain god Baal were all dead. Slaughtered in the valley. If such a god had any power, now he should truly hold back his blessing.

Ah, but Baal was powerless.

And Elijah's God? He was just getting started.

Elijah smiled. At last. At long, long last. It was all turning around. Finally. The nightmare was over.

Elijah stumbled up the mountain. He weaved between the rocky outcroppings. When he reached the summit, he fell to his knees. He buried his face into the dust at the edge of the glassy bowl where once had stood an altar restored.

To his right, the altar to Baal had been torn down. The people had burned the already-rotting sacrifice that had been left untouched. Not as a sacrifice, but to get rid of the stench. The mountaintop was deserted now. Everyone was below, camped out, waiting to see what would happen next.

And Elijah knew what had to happen next. Baal was defeated. God was triumphant. Now, now the drought must end.

He cried out.

The people had turned back to God. The king had been shamed. Send the rain.

The sky was still blue. The late afternoon sky was bare of clouds, bare of anything that indicated moisture.

Please. Please send the rain.

He groaned at the intensity of the prayer.

Rahim finally arrived, climbing up the mountain after Elijah. He sat and watched from nearby, his eyes wide.

Finally, Elijah croaked, "Go. Go look toward the sea."

Rahim scampered away, over to the other side of the summit, to stand on the edge of a cliff. He looked over the waters. The sun stared back at him, turning orange as it plunged toward the horizon. The wind blew into his eyes, causing them to water. He shivered in the cool.

He returned. "There is nothing," he said.

Elijah groaned again. No. God had won. The nightmare was over. Of course it was over. There was nothing holding him back now from showering blessing, from showering rain on his chosen people. Send the rain, God. It's time. Send relief.

"Go. Look again."

Again Rahim ran. Again he returned. Again nothing.

Again the groaning. The prophet's fists shook in his effort. The man who had prayed fire from the sky begged for water.

A third time, the boy ran. A third time, he returned with nothing to report.

And a fourth time. He wasn't running now.

The fifth time, he walked. He returned to a prophet who had just won the most wondrous victory. Who knelt beside the monument of what he had done, the glassy crater.

The sixth time, he nearly didn't come back. He couldn't stand to see this man broken so. This man who had raised him to life. This man who had taught his mother how to smile again. This man who could work miracles.

The seventh time Rahim looked out over the sea, something blotted out a corner of the nearly setting sun.

The seventh time, he sprinted back to the prophet. "A cloud! A cloud as small as a man's hand is rising from the sea!"

The prophet sat up. Tears streaked over his dirty cheeks. Something had loosened in his chest. "Go quick. Tell Ahab to hitch up his chariot. Go down before the rain stops you."

The wind came first, roaring from the west. The sky had been turning brilliant orange and red as the sun descended, but now it turned black.

The rain pounded against the mountain.

Everyone fled back to their homes to take advantage of the rain. Now they could plant. Now something could grow. Now they could at last break the hard, hard ground!

But the prophet stayed behind on the mountain. Water filled the glassy bowl beside him. He raised his dusty face to the sky. The water pounded his skin clean, clean at last. The dirt ran off him in rivulets. His dust-colored beard turned white. His dust-colored skin turned tan. The dirt flowed off him. His robe clung to him. Sheets and sheets of cold rain refreshed him, chilled him, but still he stood on the mountaintop, his face to the sky.

And the knots in his chest from years of hiding, the tension he had carried for so long, the responsibility of holding closed the sky, it all released.

They won. They finally won. Baal defeated. Humiliated. Seen for the nothing he was. The people claiming to worship God again. Victory.

Elijah had forgotten what it was like to laugh.

Chapter Ten

The king dripped water onto the tile of the palace's entrance. Thank Baal it was only water and not blood. No, only water. Precious water. The chariot could not outrun the thunderhead. It had burst on them as they raced along the stony road back to Samaria, washing over them like a wall. His chariot driver had laughed and lifted his face to the deluge. Ahab, though, had quickly smothered his surprise and joy at the rain. He pressed his lips into a tight line and scowled as he rode through the storm.

And Elijah's brat had hitched a ride, too. The child had started asking questions. Ahab had glared at him, and the whelp had shut his mouth. Ahab's thunder was far more menacing than the storm above. Still, the child annoyed him.

And an annoyed Ahab rarely meant good things for the source of his annoyance.

Elijah waited for him in the broad antechamber of the palace with a huge smile. He offered a shallow bow. "Oh King, welcome home!"

The servants had lit oil lamps and placed them on lampstands awaiting their master's arrival. The flames reflected from the highly polished marble floor. The light flickered across Ahab's dripping face.

The king eyed the prophet. "I thought you stayed behind on the mountain."

"I did."

The king glanced outside at his chariot and back at the prophet. "We left you behind there."

"You did."

And the brat burst into laughter. "You outran the chariot?"

"I did!" Elijah flung his arms open wide, and the child ran into his embrace. They laughed together.

Ahab tensed, his face flushed with fury at this insufferable prophet.

But then a woman's laughter filled the entry hall. Rich tones of mirth gushed from a side room, and then she was there. The queen.

"Oh, mighty king!" she exclaimed and approached him.

He bowed. He knew who the power was here.

Her delicious smile greeted him. "Baal has finally overcome the Hebrew God. Do you hear the rain?" She leaned back, savoring the pounding sound from the roof.

Ahab dripped on the marble floor.

"And you have brought my prophets home in triumph, have you?" She cupped his cheek in her perfect hand. "And you allow the defeated prophet to walk free among us? Have you so humiliated him we need not worry about him again?"

Ahab told her everything.

Jezebel did not take it well.

"May the gods deal with me, be it ever so severely, if by this time tomorrow I don't make your life like one of my prophets!"

Elijah fled for his life.

He ran south. Rahim followed his every step.

"Why didn't you just call on your God to defeat the queen?"

"Didn't the king finally believe in your God?"

"Aren't you going to stop the rain if they still don't believe?"

Elijah didn't answer. He couldn't. Defeat welded his jaw shut. He couldn't open his mouth to speak. He could barely open his mouth to take a swallow of water. He didn't want to eat. He wanted to lie down and die.

But the boy.

Amrah had entrusted him to the prophet.

The dust of the earth had become a thick paste of mud. Streams gurgled beside the road. If the boy wasn't asking his endless questions, he was splashing. He stared at the rushing waters, poked his finger in them, laughed. "Was there always water like this before?"

"Is this what it was like with Noah and his flood?"

"How do people learn how to swim?"

When Elijah didn't answer, the boy shrugged.

Of course. How many men had his mother brought home who never answered the boy's questions? Why should Elijah be any different from them?

He wasn't any better.

No. He was worse. They didn't know any better. Him? He worshiped the true God.

But he wasn't good enough, was he? He had given everything. Everything he had. And he had finally found victory. Rain had returned. Look at the land. Soon it would be as green as he remembered. Soon joy would flow as food grew again. As people remembered what it was to feast. The nightmare was supposed to be over. God had given a great sign. Elijah had shown the people who the true God was.

But it wasn't enough. The queen still wanted him dead. He was still alone. The last prophet, wasn't he? Alone. Just like when he was by the brook with the ravens. Just like when he was with the widow whose son died. Just like now.

The boy followed him. He deserved someone better. Someone who would teach him. Someone who would take care of him. Someone who wasn't a failure. Not this dried husk of a man who failed to represent a God strong enough to send fire and rain from the same sky.

They marched on for miles. Days. Rahim continued to delight in a land turning green under the rains.

"What kind of plant is this?"

"Why are all the plants green?"

"Can I eat this?"

Elijah continued in silence.

Finally, they stumbled into a muddy town, so small it wasn't even walled. Elijah dropped himself next to the town well. The boy hopped around, looking at everything.

A woman came to the well to draw water.

"Hello," the boy said.

The woman smiled. "Hello."

"We're going that way." The boy pointed.

The woman raised an eyebrow. "That way? There's nothing that way. Just desert."

Just desert.

Elijah couldn't take him into the wilderness. It wouldn't be right. He forced his jaws apart. "Rahim, stay here." The words fell heavily from his lips.

"Why?"

"Because."

The woman looked up from her jar at the prophet. The boy looked at him.

He could not bear the weight of their stares.

"No. Don't stay here. Go north. Go home, Rahim. I can't take care of you anymore. I can't watch you. I can't answer your questions. I'm not good enough."

The boy blinked at him.

"Here." Elijah reached inside his belt and took out a purse. He handed it to the boy. He looked at the woman. "There's enough coin there to get him home. If there is anyone trustworthy traveling north, will you see the boy goes with them?"

The woman blinked at him.

But Elijah hardly waited for an answer. "Be safe, Rahim." He turned away. He could not watch the boy. He could not hold his gaze.

He set his face south.

Into the wilderness.

Alone.

Chapter Eleven

The rain swallowed him. Sheets of it fell from a gray sky. It ran over the surface of the cracked ground. His sandals soaked through. His feet ached with the chill of it. His robe clung to him, cold leather against cold skin. Before, the rain had brought only joy. Now, though . . . Now his face was downcast. Now his heart struggled within him. Now the darkness came out to play.

Still, he set his face to the south. Into the desert. Into the wilderness.

After an hour, the sky cleared. The sun burned down at him. The desert bloomed. Green things grew. It was so green it hurt Elijah's eyes. Bushes put out leaves. Flowers burst around him in riots of color. Trees blossomed. The scent of it smothered him. He almost gagged at the power of it.

He walked on. His robe dried. It stuck to his shoulders. It weighed him down. His skin itched and prickled. Above, a bird circled. He looked up. A raven?

No. A vulture.

Well, it could have its meal soon enough. Not yet, but soon.

A day he plodded.

The darkness of his heart whispered at him. Not good enough to rescue a nation. Not even good enough to take care of a boy. Not good enough. Failure. Alone. Last. Couldn't leave anyone behind to be a prophet after him. The broken link in a chain that reached back to Moses. Sure, he had spoken the word God had given him. But he had been so weak that even the power of God wasn't enough.

Baal didn't even exist, and it had defeated the prophet.

He had failed, like generations before him. Like all the prophets who had failed to turn Israel back to the Lord. But they had some success, didn't they? Those names were still remembered, weren't they? But Elijah would only be remembered as the failure. As the last one. There would be no more after him. Never again would the Word of the Lord shatter hearts. Never again would the people be turned back to their God.

He kept shifting his robe. He had never noticed how itchy it was before. How hot it was. It almost burned his skin, it seemed. The camel hair marked him as different, for anyone who cared to look. And what had the difference gotten him? Was it worth it?

Well, he knew *he* wasn't worth it.

He stumbled. A broom tree, a massive bush, stood before him. Tiny yellow buds grew on the branches. The ground under its shade was still thick mud. A cool spot to take refuge from the light.

At last, he could push words through his lips. "I have had enough, Lord," he gasped. "Take my life. I'm no better than my ancestors." No better than all the others who had turned their backs on God. No better.

And as the prayer died on his lips, his grief overcame him. The darkness of his heart slowed his breathing. Black crept into the edges of his vision. He shut his eyes. What was there worth seeing in this broken world?

He slept at last under the branches of the broom tree.

A hand shook his shoulder.

Elijah jerked awake. His heart thundered. His breath came in bursts. Ahab. Ahab had found him!

But no. This was no evil king. This was no agent of Jezebel. Elijah did not recognize the being that had touched him, but he knew the being was pure in a way he could not fathom. He felt every bit of filth on him. Every bit of filth in him. As if he needed help with that.

The angel offered a smile. "Get up and eat." The being gestured.

There, near where Elijah's head had been, lay some hot coals, nestled in a depression in the mud. A flat cake of bread lay on them, crisping at the edges. Next to the coals sat a clay jug.

With a shaking hand, Elijah reached for the jug and lifted it to his mouth. Cool water greeted his cracked lips. He felt its soothing trickle run down his throat. He reached for the bread and tore off a chunk. It crunched between his teeth. It was good, sweet, a little like honey. It had a flavor that Amrah's bread never had. Something full about it, as if eating the full loaf would keep you satisfied for days.

God had provided. Again. Even though he had failed. Even though he was the last.

His stomach was satisfied in a way it had not been, even when he had been well provided for. His heart, though, was still hollow, and in that hollowness, the darkness dwelled. The darkness overwhelmed him again. He slept.

Again, the hand shook his shoulder. "Get up and eat. The journey is too much for you."

More cool water. More bread.

More generosity Elijah did not deserve. God should not be showing this grace.

Grace? What grace was this? To be the last? To be alone? To be a failure? To be shown pity like this? To be ground into the dirt again and again. Ravens and death and victory snatched away. And above, the vulture still circled, waiting.

Elijah stumbled to his feet. The sun hurt his eyes, but who cared about pain now? What more could be done to him? The scents of the blooming desert washed over him like incense, but this was no temple.

He staggered south. South, to die. That would be the last meal God would provide for a broken man like him, Elijah was sure. Why should God support a prophet like him? A broken, broken prophet. A prophet who came to resent the God who had given so much.

Elijah plodded through the wilderness. The sand burned through the soles of his sandals. The sun heated his shoulders and the top of his head. The vulture followed. The natural incense seeped into his pores. It was all he could smell. He walked until the sun descended to his right.

That night, he lay under the stars that were supposed to show the countless people who would worship God in purity and truth. God had promised to Abraham, hadn't he? Hundreds of years before this, God had told Abraham that as countless as the stars, as countless as sand on the seashore, his descendants would be.

Lies.

Elijah was the last one, and now he would die. And yes, there might be others who knew God. Rahim did. Amrah. Perhaps a few Obadiah said he sheltered. But how long would they continue without a prophet to speak God's Word to them? Without that Word to nourish their souls? No. The Word was leaving this world.

And this world deserved it. It had turned its back on God.

Elijah looked up at the stars. Somewhere, an owl hooted. He breathed deeply in the cool night air. He had walked a day. One day traveling through the wilderness on a jug of water and a cake of bread.

This was the end. There was no way he would be strong enough to continue under the hot sun tomorrow. The vulture would find him at last.

But the dawn came, and Elijah opened his eyes. He was still alive.

Of course he was. Why wouldn't he be alive? Why wouldn't his God mock him and keep even the rest of death from him?

No jug of water this morning. No cake of bread. Just more endless desert.

And so he went south again, the sun baking him, the sand burning him. The green began to fade into brown. The scent of incense vanished, and the familiar taste of dust replaced it. Again, he lay down when the sun had set. Again, the stars shone on him.

And again, he awoke in the morning.

The darkness in his heart flared up. Why would God do this? Why would God steal even his death from him? God had taken his ceremonial cleanliness from him when he sent the ravens. He had taken joy when the boy died. He had stolen victory. Why not death, too?

A third day passed in the wilderness. He heard no beat of horses' hooves. No dust from chariots rose to the sky. No; no one chased after him. Not even the voice of a boy who asked too many questions broke the silence.

Good. Silence was good. That meant even God was not speaking to him or through him now. Elijah hoped he forgot how to talk. He could not speak for God if he did not know how to communicate. How much easier it would be. If death was taken from him, if he was to be the last, an undying prophet of a forgotten God, at least he could be alone.

A fourth day.

A fifth.

The wilderness never ended, did it? As barren as his soul. Even the buzzards finally abandoned him. They knew he would not die.

Elijah hoped they were wrong.

A sixth day. Was it the Sabbath? Was it a day of rest? There should be a day of rest here, shouldn't there? The days of sand and stone had scrubbed away the passage of time. But he had been away from worship for so long, did it matter? Should he try to keep the Sabbath?

A seventh day.

An eighth.

Now he knew he had been walking through a Sabbath. He had to have. Still God did not let him die. His mouth was so, so dry, but his body kept going. His sandals were still firm. His clothing had not worn out. Not yet, at least.

He wept at night. The stars watched him. The angel did not return.

Ten days.

Fifteen.

How much farther would God allow him to go? Did the world end? Would he someday come to a cliff that fell into *sheol*, into the land of the dead? Could he simply walk there, never die, but at last be at rest? Oh, what a marvelous thought. To finally be at rest. And what a punishment: To not even know death, but to be dead? To walk alive into *sheol*?

The wind pushed against him as he walked, urging him along. He followed the urging.

Twenty days.

Twenty-five.

Ever south.

Thirty days. He caught the vague scent of salt water. The hills had become so much higher. Stone jutted out from the earth.

Thirty-five.

Forty days.

It was a holy number. The number of years Elijah's ancestors had wandered in the desert. The number of days it had rained for Noah.

Rain. The thought stung him. They had proven Baal false, they had won. Yet the king still rejected God, still rejected Elijah. And yet God had sent rain anyway. Was it still raining there? Had the mud swallowed them all? Would the waters rise and cleanse the earth of the filth they had brought on it?

Ah, but God was faithful. He had promised: never again would there be a flood that would wipe out all of mankind.

Pity.

And then Elijah looked up. A peak blotted out the sky. He had never been here before. Never before had he gone so far. But he knew with the certainty of a prophet.

This was the place where God had given the Ten Commandments. The place where he had descended and spoken to the people hundreds of years before. The place where he had spoken to a much greater prophet, a man named Moses. Moses had been on this mountain for forty days.

This was the mountain of God.

Chapter Twelve

The stones burned the palms of his hands as he climbed. The sun glared at his back as he hauled himself up the peak. Finally, there, a cave. He crawled into it, collapsing. He heaved for breath as he lay on the stone floor, looking up at a jagged ceiling. The darkness of the cave swallowed him whole as the sun descended, sending longer and longer shadows. The cold nibbled at his fingertips, his toes, and finally devoured him. The darkness in his heart met the darkness in the cave and laughed at him.

Maybe at last he would be allowed to die. Here, on holy ground, the useless prophet would die of the cold.

He let sleep take him, perhaps never to wake.

But dawn awakened him anyway.

He breathed in incense. Not the natural incense of a desert in bloom, but something holy in a way that made every other scent of the world ashamed to call itself beautiful. He opened his eyes. The darkness of the cave was broken by indirect light shining from its mouth. He had an overpowering urge to take off his sandals.

The word of the Lord came to him. "What are you doing here, Elijah?"

When God speaks, he speaks with such reality that is impossible to lie to him. The darkness in Elijah's heart leaped through his mouth. "I have been very zealous for the Lord God Almighty. But the Israelites? Your chosen people? They rejected your covenant! They broke down your altars! Your prophets? They put them to death! And me?" The words flooded out of him. So many years of pent-up rage. So much brokenness. All of it pouring out of his heart, all at once. "Me? I'm the last prophet. They're trying to kill me, too."

The Lord answered, "Elijah. Go out and stand on the mountain in the presence of the Lord, for the Lord is about to pass by."

Elijah's hands curled into fists. He trembled, but not with holy fear.

God hadn't answered him. Elijah had poured out his heart, and what was God going to do? Get revenge on Ahab at last? Strike down that treacherous nation he'd chosen? None of that. No. Instead, God was going to pass by?

And then wind shrieked past the mouth of the cave. Elijah hurled himself to the ground. He had never heard such a sound. It sounded like the wind itself had gone to war against the mountains, clawing at every crevice, tearing them apart. Peaks shattered like clay jars.

Yes. This was the rage that should be aimed at Israel. This was what they deserved! Turn this fury on Ahab and all those who had tried to kill Elijah, who had forced him out, who had caused such grief! If God wouldn't destroy the world in water, let him destroy it in wind!

But as Elijah listened, he did not hear God in the wind.

The howling died down. Rocks clattered down the peaks and came to rest. Elijah heard his own breathing again.

Then the floor of the cave lurched. Elijah tumbled through the air. Dust rained down on him. The earth itself gave way. The wind had shown power, but this? To turn the very ground you stood on into an enemy?

Yes, God. Use this, then. Like you turned the ground into a hungry mouth to swallow up those who rebelled against Moses so long ago. Show your displeasure! Turn it against those rebellious ones who rejected me! You, I mean! They rejected you!

Even as Elijah struggled to find safety, even as he imagined the ground opening its mouth to swallow Ahab whole, he felt that God was not in the earthquake.

The rumblings ceased. The ground again was tamed. Finally, again, all was still. Elijah heard his heartbeat but not the movement of the earth.

Another sound came from outside the cave. A great gasping sound, but with it came crackling. And heat. And light.

Elijah's skin broke out in sweat. He had felt the heat of the wilderness on the journey here. He had thought that heat was enough. But this? This was so much more. The sun itself bent to kiss the earth with its fury. This rage smothered him. It was so, so hard to breathe.

But this was better yet. Let those who rejected God feel the fire of his rage. Let it rain down on them like it had rained down on the altar on Mount Carmel! Elijah closed his eyes against the light and heat and prayed that God would turn against his enemies.

But God was not in the fire.

The light dimmed. Elijah remembered what coolness felt like again. The fire was gone.

And then came a whisper. It was not the angry whisper of a mother to shush her too-loud child. It was not the dangerous whisper of someone about to explode in anger. No. It was a gentle, gentle whisper of a mother rocking her child to sleep.

And there. There was God.

And there, Elijah at last felt fear. If he was going to die, well, he was ready for it. He had begged for it. He had longed to walk alive into *sheol*. But when someone comes with gentleness, there is so much to fear. Elijah covered his face with his cloak. He knew what the Law said: Those who see the face of God will die. Only those with clean hearts may approach God and live.

And Elijah, well, his heart was not clean.

With his face covered so he could not even see the nature of the light outside, he stumbled to the mouth of the cave.

And the smell of God—that perfect incense smell—grew, but it did not overpower. Its aroma opened a yearning in Elijah that he had never known he felt before. A longing to merely breathe in the goodness of God. To stand and inhale it would be enough. To taste the mercy of God, like bread and wine, like running water on a hot day.

And the goodness was too much for him. The darkness lashed out. How could God pretend to be so good when he allowed Ahab to rule his chosen people? How could God imagine himself to be that pure when he allowed his prophet to suffer so much?

And that gentle, gentle whisper spoke to him. "What are you doing here, Elijah?"

God asked him the same question again?

How dare he? How *dare* God ask a question like that? He knew very well why Elijah was here. He knew the failures. He knew how he had humiliated Elijah again and again. He knew how broken he was. He knew all of that, and he dare ask Elijah that question? What was he doing here?

And all the anger he felt before flared back. The darkness within him lashed out. God asked the same question? He would get the same answer. "I have been very zealous for the Lord God Almighty!" So zealous he was willing to live unclean by a brook for months. To be fed by ravens. To be alone for so long. To live outside of God's Promised Land. To live with an unclean woman and her unclean son. To fail and be hunted and be haunted by all he had failed to do. "The Israelites have rejected your covenant, broken down your altars, and put your prophets to death with the sword. And me? I am the only one left. And now they're trying to kill me, too!"

Let God answer that. Let him face the wrath of man for once. Let him provide answers for what he had done!

But that is not the way God answers. Not even to his chosen prophet. Not even to the man he called for his own purposes. Not even to a broken man like Elijah.

God answered, but not the way Elijah expected.

"Go back the way you came. Go to the desert of Damascus. When you get there, anoint Hazael king over Aram. Also, anoint Jehu son of Nimshi king over Israel."

Elijah heard what God said. And his heart thrilled.

God had chosen a new king, and it was not Ahab's son. This Jehu, whoever that was, would be king over Israel now. God had spoken.

No. Not just spoken. He had heard. He had heard Elijah's cry.

And this Jehu—surely he could be no worse than Ahab, could he? How could he? It would be a new beginning in Israel. At last, at last God's people would begin again. And if Elijah was to anoint him, perhaps he would have some sway over him. Perhaps he could point the king to God. Perhaps goodness might return.

Even as all these thoughts raced through Elijah, God continued, "And anoint Elisha son of Shaphat from Abel Meholah to succeed you as prophet."

Anoint Elisha to succeed you as prophet.

Another prophet.

Under his cloak, Elijah wept.

He was not the last.

No, he was not the last. God had chosen someone to follow him. God did not answer why. God did not answer Elijah's anger. He did something better: He said there would be another after him. That even in all his failures, there would be another. That the chain was not broken. That though he was unworthy, that though God's people had rejected him, God would continue to speak to them. His Word would not die. He would also send another prophet. Someone better than Elijah. Oh, please. Let him be better than Elijah.

God continued, "Jehu will put to death any who escape the sword of Hazael, and Elisha will put to death any who escape the sword of Jehu."

There. God's rage would not be held back forever. Elijah might not see it, but the ones he anointed would see it done. The Lord had not abandoned his people. He would come in righteous fury. He would make things right.

God still spoke. "Yet I reserve seven thousand in Israel—all whose knees have not bowed down to Baal and all whose mouths have not kissed him."

Wait.

Wait. Elijah swallowed.

Seven thousand? There were yet seven *thousand* in Israel who trusted God's promises?

He wasn't alone.

Maybe he had failed in so many ways. No. No *maybe*. He had failed so much. But God reserved seven thousand?

God did the work. He reserved them. Elijah didn't. Elijah couldn't. It was all about what God did. It was all about him keeping his promises. He didn't need Elijah to do it, did he? It didn't depend on the prophet at all. It depended on God. Just like the stars didn't depend on Elijah, just like the sand didn't depend on him, God didn't depend on him. He kept every promise, whether through Elijah or through others.

Seven thousand? Elijah tried to imagine that many people standing together. He tried to picture it, as if they were gathered on Mount Carmel, as if they had gathered to offer a sacrifice on the altar of the Lord, as if that glassy crater was full of incense. And he tried to imagine the incense smelling to God as good as God smelled to him. He imagined them singing. What would it be like to be united in song with that many? To lift up psalms, those ancient songs of praise?

Now God had finished speaking, but for Elijah it was just the beginning of the tears. They were not tears of despair anymore, though.

No. These were tears of joy.

He was not alone.

He was not the last.

And Elijah sang with broken voice through broken lips, broken words from a broken man. He sang the psalms he remembered from his youth. He pictured those seven thousand around him. He was not alone.

And he would teach the psalms to another. He was not the last.

And over and over through the day, at the mouth of that cave, wind-shattered, earth-shaken, fire-burned, Elijah wept as he remembered what God had said.

He was not alone.

He was not the last.

Chapter Thirteen

The journey home took him back through the wilderness. The sandy-red mountains gave way to endless plains of wilderness.

This time, the darkness of his heart stayed away for the most part. It would emerge on occasion, but Elijah clung to the truth: He was not alone. He was not the last. God himself had said it, and God did not know how to lie. It was so foreign to him; he hated anything that was not true. And if God said it, it did not matter what his heart said. The darkness inside him lied.

And for now, at least, the darkness could not overpower him.

Elijah had been gone for almost three months by the time he reached Israel. And in that time, the rain had fallen. Crops were growing. Farmers were harvesting. In fact, the first harvest was done, and many farmers were planting a second crop. Laughter had returned.

He stood in a field, mystified. Had it ever been like this before?

And there. A line of oxen, each pair pulling a plow. Men urged the oxen on, pressing down on their implements, breaking up the softened soil. Elijah heard snatches of song here and there among the men. Their bass voices carried across the field. Even at this distance, Elijah heard their joy, but he could not recognize the words.

No. No, Elijah did recognize them.

They were singing a psalm.

> "You crown the year with your bounty,
> And your carts overflow with abundance.
> The grasslands of the desert overflow,
> The hills are clothed with gladness.
> The meadows are covered with flocks
> And the valleys are mantled with grain;
> They shout for joy and sing."

What was this? Was this the Israel Elijah had fled? How could it be? God's discipline had not shaken them. His miracle of fire had not truly changed them. But his grace? His sending the rain when they did not deserve it?

Grace changed their hearts?

Elijah's eyes grazed over the men driving the plows and settled on the man at the end of the line. He felt a smile bloom on his face. The man drove out the song with the same passion he drove his yoke. Though the hair on the sides of his head was still black, he was bald on the top of his head. His cheeks were red with effort.

Elisha. The man who would follow him.

The prophet made his way across the field, across the rich black soil, across the moist ground, to the man who sang as he drove his oxen on. Sweat soaked through his robe. Elijah took off his cloak and threw it over the man's shoulders. Elijah kept walking. Let's see who this man is who would be the next prophet.

Elisha's song died away. He looked at the cloak. He looked up after Elijah. He took in the strange clothes: Camel hair. Thick leather belt. He looked back down at the cloak on his shoulders, his mind grinding at what had just happened.

Elisha looked up suddenly. It dawned on him: The prophet was choosing him. He would "take up the mantle." He startled and dropped the plow he was holding, his eyes bright. He chased after the prophet and called out, "Just let me kiss my father and mother goodbye. Then I'll come with you!"

"Go back." Elijah shook his head. "What have I done to you?"

Elisha jumped. He whooped to the sky. He ran back.

The farmer thought being a prophet would be wonderful. He must. Why else would he rejoice to be someone like Elijah? Someone hated? Someone who hid for years and years, only to be hunted? Elijah shook his head. This man had no idea what was going to happen to him, did he? He had no idea the struggle he would encounter. How amazing and how terrifying it was.

It was not such a simple thing, to be someone who spoke for God. Someone who heard God's own voice.

No. This new prophet, this one who was marked to follow him, he was a fool, wasn't he?

Elijah shook his head. He was still a fool himself, for that matter. An older fool now, surely. A fool who had traveled so far. A fool who believed lies more often than not. But perhaps even a fool could learn. Perhaps.

Elisha, though, didn't go back to his father and mother. He went to the oxen he'd been driving. He took the yoke off of them.

The other workers in the field kept moving. Once an ox started moving, it was best to take advantage of it. They drove on across the field, toward Elijah now. The plows bit into rich earth. The oxen grunted and strained. The men did the same.

Elisha took his oxen, there in the middle of the field, and slaughtered them. He ran to a nearby stand of trees and gathered kindling. Everything he did was fast. He moved with a vigor Elijah didn't think he'd ever possessed. He brought the kindling, laid it under the yoke, and lit it all on fire. The oxen served as a sacrifice.

The fire cooked the meat. By the time he had done all this, the other eleven pair of oxen had been driven back down the field and put to rest. The bald man laughed. "Come and eat!" he proclaimed.

The other men looked at each other. At Elisha.

One sputtered, "What are you doing?"

"I'm not coming back here. I won't need the yoke or the oxen ever again." He slipped the cloak over his shoulders. "I'm going to be a prophet."

"You?"

Elijah spied his grin, even across the field. "Me! Now eat. Call your families. Enjoy it, all of you. What was mine is now yours, for now I belong to the Lord!" He whooped again, jumping up and down. And then he sprinted across the field to where Elijah sat, waiting. He skidded to a halt.

Dirt under his fingernails. Mud staining his shins. His robe was girded so he was prepared to work. Sweat dripped off of him. He breathed so hard.

"Master. I'm ready."

Elijah raised an eyebrow. "Are you now? Well. Let's go." And with that, he hauled himself to his feet with a groan and set out.

Yes. This young one was foolish, but perhaps the best prophets were fools. And perhaps Elijah could learn from his enthusiasm.

Elisha followed after.

And just like that, what God had promised was made true. Elijah was not alone. He was not the last. Not anymore.

Chapter Fourteen

And for years, Elisha watched and learned from Elijah. He experienced how good the aroma of God was. He learned how to suffer for God's name. He saw the power of the one they served. All in all, he learned what it was to be a prophet of the living God.

Ahab died. Jezebel died. The next king died. It was amazing how little changed. It was like the kings were unable to listen to God's prophets.

But despite that, prophets returned to the land. Not every prophet was like Elijah. Not every single one heard God's voice. Many simply knew what God had caused to be written and were able to share what God had told generations past and apply it to people today. Elisha learned much from them, gobbling up everything he could about the God who had chosen someone like Elijah and someone like him.

Every once in a while, Elijah would call him Rahim. Elisha asked who that was, but Elijah wouldn't say. Elisha never learned about the boy who was left behind.

Elisha never expected he would be left behind, too.

Dawn. Elisha chewed on some bread left from the day before as he gazed out over the city of Gilgal, where he and Elijah had been staying. Elijah climbed down from the upstairs room. The two of them watched the east together in silence. Elijah breathed in the scent of the bread, of the recently-stirred fire. "Stay here, Elisha. God has sent me to Bethel."

Elisha answered, "As surely as the Lord lives, I will not leave you." He turned to look at his master. He absorbed it all. The white beard. The wrinkled face, hard as leather. He set that face in his memory.

Elijah shook his head, a smile in the corner of his mouth. Perhaps Elisha knew. "Well. Come, then."

Together, they journeyed east. They talked along the way about all Elijah had learned. What God had told him. How he had struggled with the darkness in his heart.

"You still struggle with it," Elisha said.

"Yes. I do. But I have learned that the darkness lies. I was never alone. And I was never the last. And even though I failed, God showed me so much patience." Elijah shook his head. "He kept every promise. Like you." Elijah patted his disciple on the shoulder. "You are a promise fulfilled. I didn't think I would ever have someone like you. And some days I still think you will run from me. You should have many times."

Elisha laughed. "Well. I haven't yet."

"Not yet." Elijah looked on down the road as they walked. "I have learned that my heart lies. And someday I will learn the lesson and not forget it. Maybe today." He raised his eyes to the blue, blue sky. "Maybe today."

They reached Bethel, and a company of prophets came out to meet them. They greeted Elijah warmly. They all knew him, of course. Elijah nearly wept. To be recognized as the one who spoke God's Word during those dark days? How could they show him such respect? He was nothing. Nothing at all.

He still marveled that so many worshiped God openly. How could this be? From the days when they had all fled, when he had thought he was the last—and now, to be surrounded by such a great company of witnesses, to be respected? He shouldn't be. And yet, here they were. Evidence he was not alone, and that Elisha would never be alone. He would never know that kind of darkness.

And as many men spoke with Elijah, a few prophets pulled Elisha aside. One said, "Do you know that the Lord is going to take your master away today?"

Suddenly, Elisha couldn't speak. He cleared his throat. "Yes, I know. Don't . . . Don't speak of it."

"Elisha!" The broken prophet came up behind him. "Stay here. The Lord has sent me to Jericho."

And Elisha forced a grin. "As surely as the Lord lives, I will not leave you."

"Ha! Then come. It is time to depart."

And so they left the prophets of Bethel and continued on the road east. A raven settled on a tree as they approached. It cawed at them. It fluffed out its wings, and a few dark feathers fluttered to the ground.

Elijah paused and pondered the feathers. He shook his head. He pointed. "I'm not enough, Elisha. Never forget that. But God used me anyway. Did I ever tell you about how I ran away? For over a month?"

"You have. Many times."

"Don't forget. I'm a failure. I'm broken."

Elisha gripped his mentor's arms. "You've blessed me."

"Only because you're fool enough to follow me."

The younger man shrugged. "Maybe. Your singing is horrible."

Elijah barked a laugh. The raven in the tree glided away. They continued their journey. As they went, they sang together. It didn't matter that Elijah couldn't sing two notes that sounded good next to each other. In Elisha's ears, his praise was as pleasing as meat roasting on a fire.

Elisha found he had a hard time singing, though. His voice grew thicker with every step. Elijah only sang louder to carry them along.

They reached Jericho. The great city on the hill overlooked the Jordan River. A steep incline took their road down to the river far below. But from the city, a group of men came out to meet them. More prophets.

More prophets. Enough for two cities. More than Elijah had ever dreamed. They came and paid their respects to the great prophet. Elijah greeted them all warmly.

A few pulled Elisha aside. "Do you know?" they asked. "The Lord is going to take your master from you today."

The younger man didn't answer for a few moments. Finally, he replied, "I know. Do not speak of it."

"Elisha." The old man's voice had become soft as he approached. "Elisha, stay here. The Lord has called me to the Jordan."

And the young man forced a smile again. "As surely as the Lord lives, I will not leave you."

The old man searched his face for a moment. He nodded. "Of course. Then come. It is time to go."

Fifty of the prophets came with them.

Fifty of them.

How could that be? Elijah had been alone. But he'd been wrong, hadn't he? God had not left him alone. Not truly. There were so many that worshiped the true God.

Not alone.

Not the last.

They came to the river. The Jordan was at flood stage, a raging torrent of snowmelt from much farther upstream. Elisha gazed at the rushing waters. "Well, we're here."

"Not yet." Elijah slipped off his cloak and laid it out on the dusty ground. As Elisha looked on, the prophet rolled up the fabric. He came to the edge of the water and used the cloth as an awkward whip. The fabric struck the water.

And the water ran away. The fierce river stopped what it was doing. The rapids stood still. The water separated to the left and to the right, leaving a dry path to the other side. Elijah turned, a smile playing at his lips. He unfurled his cloak, slipped it back on, and made his way across.

Elisha rushed after.

The old prophet climbed the opposite bank. As soon as Elisha hauled himself over the other side, the waters splashed. The torrent resumed. The spray refreshed them.

Elijah gave a deep sigh. "The prophets over there. They told you."

"Yes." Elisha paused. "They didn't need to, though."

"Well." The old prophet looked around at the hills, at the sky, at the river. "Tell me. What can I do for you before I am taken from you?"

"Let me inherit a double portion of your spirit," the younger man answered.

Elijah felt his eyebrows rise. Really? Elisha knew all of the suffering he'd gone through. He knew his misery. His loneliness. Why would anyone want a double portion of that?

But it wasn't just that, was it? God had blessed him, too. And that's what Elisha saw. He saw the respect. He saw how things had turned out. And he wanted that.

Elijah offered a sad smile. "Well. You've asked a difficult thing." He swallowed. "But if you see me when I am taken from you, it will be yours. Otherwise not." His eyes flicked to the hills. "Come. It is not time yet."

And they climbed the other side of the Jordan Valley. The other prophets looked on from beyond the river. The two men chatted, mostly about nothing. It is always hard to talk when you know something great is about to happen.

Elijah stopped and breathed deeply. "Do you smell that?" The aroma stilled his heart. It was good in a way he ached to wrap himself in.

Elisha closed his eyes and inhaled.

A chariot made of fire pulled by horses of flame burst from somewhere beyond their ability to see. It came between the two of them The horses made no sound. Their hooves didn't seem to strike the ground. All the prophets could hear was the wind and the flames.

Elisha cried out, shielded his eyes, tried to get through to be with his mentor. The smell wrapped around him, even as the heat of the flames scorched him. "Elijah! Elijah!"

The prophet turned back to his disciple and grinned. And then the scent became more intense. It pushed against Elijah. No, not just the scent. The wind. Elijah felt it push through his beard. It gathered around his cloak, sending its folds fluttering. It lifted him. He cried out in surprise.

And then he began to laugh.

He felt the cloak slip off his shoulders. From somewhere beyond the rush of the winds, he heard Elisha cry out, "My father! My father! The chariots and horsemen of Israel!"

Ah. So Elisha saw. Good, then. He would be a prophet even greater than Elijah. That's what the world needed. Someone shouting God's Word in a way he never did. Sharing God's Word better than this failure, this broken prophet ever could. Someone who maybe wouldn't complain that God fed him with ravens. Someone who wouldn't run away and weep. Someone who would share what was real, what truly changed people: God's grace.

The winds grew more intense. He was lifted higher and higher into the sky. It was so bright.

And he felt his sorrows slide off his shoulders just as his cloak had. His laughter turned to tears. Oh, what a fool he had been. How selfish! How ungrateful! God had been so good to him. God had taken care of him. And now look! God was bringing him Home. He had prayed for death once, and God had not granted it. And God still would not grant that prayer.

He felt all the darkness within him leak out through his eyes. All the despair he had handed himself over to. All the doubt, the fear, the anger. It bled out of him. He thought about all the times he had been foolish with the goodness of God. How good God was. It was as if all he had ever done was spilling out through his eyes and away. He collapsed on the ground.

The ground?

And then he felt a hand on his face. Someone wiped his tears away. And with that touch, something healed his soul.

"Welcome Home, Elijah."

"You know my name," he sobbed. Oh, but it was not a sob of sorrow anymore. Now it was a sob of wonder.

"Of course I know your name." He had never heard laughter in a voice like that. Such joy in so few words. Such tenderness.

The two embraced. Elijah breathed in the scent of his robes. Oh, that goodness. He had sampled it before, but now it was so much more. It was as if he had only read about the goodness, and now he held it in his arms.

Or rather, the Goodness held Elijah in his arms.

"Come. Come to the place I have prepared for you. Well done, good and faithful servant."

"I was not faithful."

"I have taken your sins away. All that remains is your service." And he smiled at Elijah. He was actually happy to see him. He was pleased to see this broken prophet. "Come. Come and join the laughter at the feast. Come."

And Elijah did.

Elisha stared into the sky.

The broken prophet. The one who had despaired so often. And God had taken him directly to heaven. He never died. He never would.

Finally, the younger man bent and picked up the cloak. The same cloak Elijah had put on him years ago. His, now.

Well.

He turned and headed back to the river. Back to Israel.

Back to share God's Word.

About the Author

Luke Italiano has served as a pastor since 2011. He also wears the names husband, father, brother, friend, and many more.

But over all these, he is blessed to be called "Child of God." Joyfully serving the Savior who loves him, even in his brokenness. Sharing that good news with others in their brokenness. And rejoicing in the promise of a perfect heavenly home to come.

dawnsbrook.com

https://www.facebook.com/DawnsbrookPress
https://www.instagram.com/dawnsbrookpress/